The Birthday Presents

ANE FOR A'

Falkirk Council

For Anna and Katy

Text copyright © 1999 by Paul Stewart. Illustrations copyright © 1999 by Chris Riddell.
The rights of Paul Stewart and Chris Riddell to be identified as the author and illustrator
of this work have been asserted by them in accordance with the Copyright, Designs and Patents Act, 1988.
First published in Great Britain in 1999 by Andersen Press Ltd., 20 Vauxhall Bridge Road, London SW1V 2SA.
Published in Australia by Random House Australia Pty., 20 Alfred Street, Milsons Point, Sydney, NSW 2061.
This paperback edition first published in 2001 by Andersen Press Ltd. All rights reserved.
Colour separated in Italy by Fotoriproduzione Grafiche, Verona.
Printed and bound in Italy by Grafiche AZ, Verona.

10 9 8 7 6 5 4 3 2 1

British Library Cataloguing in Publication Data available.

ISBN 1 84270 035 9

This book has been printed on acid-free paper

The Birthday Presents

by Paul Stewart
with pictures by Chris Riddell

Andersen Press
London

"HEDGEHOG," said Rabbit. "When is your birthday?"
"I don't know," said Hedgehog.
Rabbit sighed. "Neither do I," he said.

"If I don't know when my birthday is,"
said Hedgehog, "how could you?"
"I mean," said Rabbit, "I don't know
when *my* birthday is."
"Ah," said Hedgehog.

As the sun sank behind the trees,
Hedgehog and Rabbit thought sadly
of all the birthdays they would never have.

"I have an idea," said Hedgehog.
"Let us celebrate our birthdays tomorrow."
"But they might not be tomorrow," said Rabbit.
"But they *might* be," said Hedgehog.
"It will be a shame to miss them if they are."

"You are right," said Rabbit. "It is a good idea.
We will wish each other Happy Birthday."
"We will give each other presents," said Hedgehog.
"Presents?" yawned Rabbit.
"Birthday presents," said Hedgehog. "That's what
birthdays are for."

LATER, as Hedgehog snuffled for slugs
beneath the plump, silver moon,
he wondered what present to give his friend.

Hedgehog thought about under-the-earth
where Rabbit was fast asleep.
"How silent and gloomy and damp it must be.
How dark!"

An empty bottle glinted down by the lake.
Hedgehog looked at the bottle.
Hedgehog looked at the moon on the water.
"That's it!" he cried.

Hedgehog filled the bottle with the bright water.

"A bottle of moonlight shall be my present," he said. Then he wrapped it up and went to bed.

RABBIT woke early, too excited to stay asleep. "What present should I give to Hedgehog?" he wondered.

Rabbit thought of his friend,
sleeping in the wide open up-there.
"How frightening and noisy it must be.
How bright!"

In the corner of his burrow,
he spied his useful tin.
"The very thing!" he cried.

Rabbit filled the tin with warm,
snuggly darkness and patted
it down with his paw.
"A box of cosiness," he said.

He pressed the lid into place

and wrapped it all up with straw.
"Hedgehog will love my present."

EVENING came. The two friends met.

"Rabbit," said Hedgehog. "Happy Birthday!"

"Hedgehog," said Rabbit. "Happy Birthday to *you*!"

"Here is a present for you," said Hedgehog.
Rabbit tore off the wrapping-leaf.
"It's a bottle of moonlight," said Hedgehog,
"so that you will no longer be afraid of the
very-very dark in your burrow."

"But I'm not . . ."
Rabbit stopped.
"Thank you," he said. "It's a wonderful present."

"And here is *your* present," said Rabbit.
Hedgehog tore off the wrapping-straw.

"It's a box of cosiness," said Rabbit,
"so that you will no longer be disturbed
by the bright, noisy day."

"But I'm not . . ."
Hedgehog stopped.
"It's just what I've always wanted," he said.

In the middle of the dark night,
Rabbit woke and looked at his present.
"Dear Hedgehog," he said.
"A bottle of moonlight, indeed!"
He took out the stopper
and drank the water inside.
"I can fill it with water every day," said Rabbit.
"Then I will never be thirsty in the night again."

AT the end of the long, rustling night,
Hedgehog noticed his present.
"Dear Rabbit," he said, sleepily.
"A box of cosiness, indeed!"
Hedghog opened the lid and looked inside.
"It's a slug-catcher!" he said.
"I will never be hungry if I wake up in the day again."

THAT evening, Hedgehog found Rabbit
down by the lake.
"Do you like your bottle of light?" he said.

"Yes," said Rabbit. "It's the best present
I've ever had. Do you like your box of cosiness?"
"Yes," said Hedgehog. "It's the best present
I've ever had."

Together, the two friends watched the sun
turn from orange to red.

"Hedgehog," said Rabbit, rubbing his eyes.
"When shall we have another birthday?"
"Soon," said Hedgehog. "Very soon."

More Andersen Press paperback picture books!

A LITTLE BIT OF WINTER
by Paul Stewart and Chris Riddell

DR. XARGLE'S BOOK OF EARTH TIGGERS
by Jeanne Willis and Tony Ross

CROCODILE'S MASTERPIECE
by Max Velthuijs

SCRAPS
by Mark Foreman

DILLY DALLY AND THE NINE SECRETS
by Elizabeth MacDonald and Ken Brown

THE PERFECT PET
by Peta Coplans

WHAT WOULD WE DO WITHOUT MISSUS MAC?
by Gus Clarke

I'LL TAKE YOU TO MRS COLE
by Nigel Gray and Michael Foreman

THAT'S MY DAD
by Ralph Steadman

MARINETTA AT THE BALLET
by Elaine Mills

WHAT'S INSIDE?
by Satoshi Kitamura

LADYBIRD, LADYBIRD
by Ruth Brown